To all the brave children
who feel overwhelmed sometimes.
You are not alone.

One Thursday Afternoon

written and illustrated by

Barbara DiLorenzo

One Thursday afternoon, Granddad picked up Ava from school.

"Hey, Ava," said Granddad.
"What's wrong, kiddo?"

"Nothing," Ava said.

"I have a little surprise for you. I packed a picnic and our paints," said Granddad.

Ava didn't answer.

After a while, they stopped
at a nature trail.

Ava sighed. "Can't we just go home?"

"Not quite yet," Granddad said.

"But I had a bad day. I just want to be alone right now," Ava said.

"That's okay. I won't talk," said Granddad. "We can both be alone. Together."

So they were quiet.
The ducks, not so much.

After their picnic, Granddad asked,
"Are you ready to paint?"

"I guess," Ava said.

"Before you use your paintbrush, Ava, use all your senses," said Granddad.

Ava kept still. She looked up at the trees. She listened for the birds, smelled the cool air, and felt the earth under her feet.

Suddenly her cheeks felt hot and her eyes felt wet.

"Granddad, I have something to say. I was so scared today. We had a lockdown drill at school. We had to hide in a safe place in our classroom. But I thought my classroom was already safe."

Granddad sat close. "That does sound scary."

"When I was your age, we had safety drills called 'Duck and Cover.' We had to hide under our desks," he said. "It was hard for us to understand. I never admitted it, but I was really scared back then. I still am sometimes."

Ava took a deep breath. "Even you?"

"Even me," said Granddad. "But, Ava, even though the world is scary, it's also a beautiful place."

"Sometimes," Ava said. "Let's paint now."

Ava felt a little better.

But as Granddad went to his easel,
she felt the sadness creep back.

"Granddad, you may have been scared in school, but did you ever see news reports of schools in danger?" she asked. "I sometimes do."

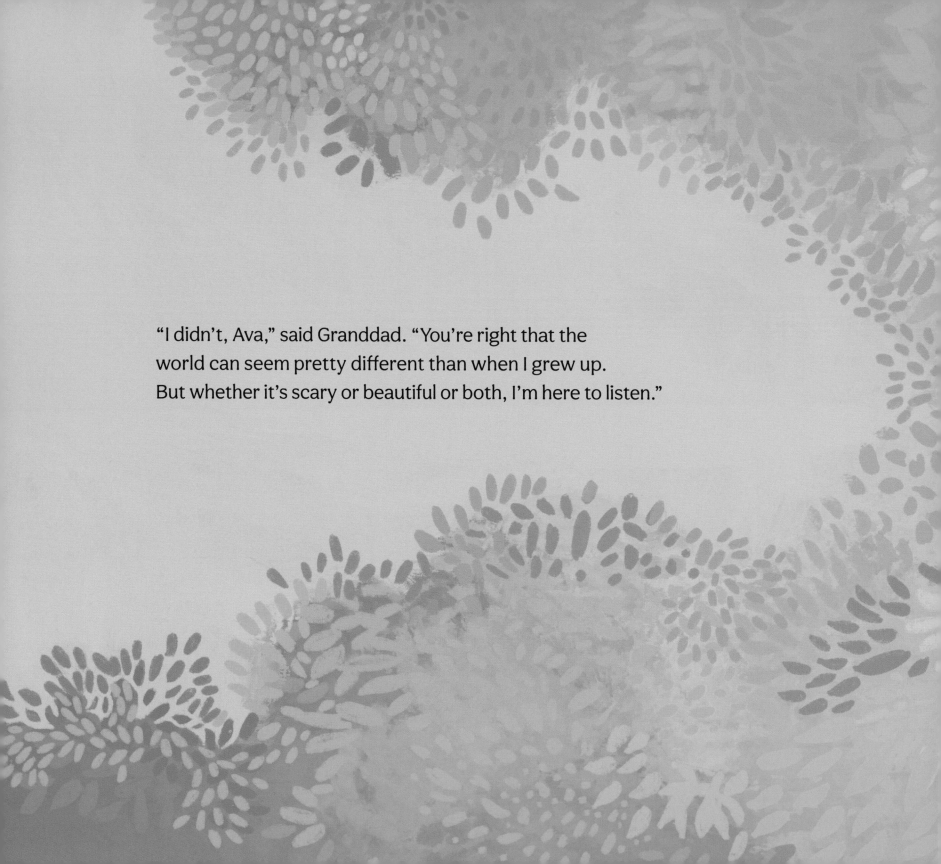

"I didn't, Ava," said Granddad. "You're right that the world can seem pretty different than when I grew up. But whether it's scary or beautiful or both, I'm here to listen."

Ava still felt a little scared,
but talking helped.

So did quiet.

And so did painting, using all her senses.

"Let's paint outside again," said Ava.
Granddad smiled. "How about tomorrow?"

As the leaves rustled and the ducks quacked,
Ava and Granddad packed up and headed home.

A Note from the Author/Illustrator

I didn't expect to create this book; I had funnier stories in mind. That changed when I experienced an actual lockdown during an author visit to an elementary school. As the adults stood chatting after my last presentation, an alarm rang—the signal for an active lockdown. The school librarian quickly locked the door, shut off the lights, and pulled the shades. We huddled in a corner for forty-five minutes, not knowing whether an intruder was in our building. I thought of the children with whom I'd been sharing my love of art and books not even an hour prior. I wondered if they were having a hard time keeping quiet, if they were thinking of what might happen, if they were as scared as I was. We later learned that there was no active threat, yet everyone felt the impact of what might have been.

For more than a year, I wrestled with the idea of creating a book prompted by this day. I kept trying to walk away from such a hard topic. Yet every news story about schools in danger renewed my sense that there was a place for a book like this. Even a preparatory lockdown drill can prompt fears of *what if?* This is just one fear kids may experience in places that should feel safe.

I wanted to validate all the feelings kids have about things that scare them. And I wanted to remind adults that our job is to listen, just as people in my life had truly listened to me. One of these people was my father. When I was a child, I loved talking with him about everything, big or small. He was always ready for a long conversation and would treat me with respect. In the spirit of my father, Granddad came into focus as a safe outlet for Ava to share her fears.

No matter how old we are, fear often comes close. What can we do when it does? In a world that may seem full of danger and anxiety, fear won't go away entirely, but fostering certain habits can help keep it in proportion. Just like Ava and Granddad, you can try to:

Listen well. Talk when you're ready.

Offer companionship. Stay close to someone you love.

Do something creative (art or music or a science experiment) using all your senses.

Spend time in nature. Breathe. Notice beauty.

As Granddad says, even though the world is scary, it is also a beautiful place. May we listen well to those around us, helping one another build resilience and courage.

Special thanks to

Katie Bruce, Mimi Bowlin, and Martha Liu of Princeton Public Library;
Shana Lindsey-Morgan and Avery Morgan; The Chapin School;
Nicole Langdo and Painted Oak Nature School; my agent, Rachel Orr;
my editor, Jeannette Larson; my art director, Allison Taylor;
my family, Jonathan Fisk, Rennie DiLorenzo, and Madison Fisk;
my childhood friends Sage Pagano, Glendon Barnes, Lex Lyon,
Beth and Lindsey Miller, and Holly Somers;
my dad, Keating Willcox

© 2022 Barbara DiLorenzo

First edition
Published by Flyaway Books
Louisville, Kentucky

22 23 24 25 26 27 28 29 30 31–10 9 8 7 6 5 4 3 2 1

Book design by Allison Taylor
Text set in Aesthet Nova

PRINTED IN CHINA

Most Flyaway Books are available at special quantity discounts when purchased in bulk by corporations, organizations, and special-interest groups. For more information, please e-mail SpecialSales@flyawaybooks.com.

Library of Congress Cataloging-in-Publication Data
Names: DiLorenzo, Barbara, author, illustrator.
Title: One Thursday afternoon / written and illustrated by Barbara DiLorenzo.
Description: First edition. | Louisville, Kentucky : Flyaway Books, [2022] | Audience: Ages 3-7. | Audience: Grades K-1. | Summary: "Granddad helps Ava process her emotions surrounding a lockdown drill at school through companionship and creativity"-- Provided by publisher.
Identifiers: LCCN 2021059585 (print) | LCCN 2021059586 (ebook) | ISBN 9781947888371 (hardback) | ISBN 9781646982561 (ebook)
Subjects: CYAC: Grandfathers--Fiction. | Emotions--Fiction. | Emergency drills--Fiction. | Schools--Fiction. | LCGFT: Picture books.
Classification: LCC PZ7.1.D5635 On 2022 (print) | LCC PZ7.1.D5635 (ebook) | DDC [E]--dc23
LC record available at https://lccn.loc.gov/2021059585
LC ebook record available at https://lccn.loc.gov/2021059586